THE WANDERING NATURE OF US GIRLS

THE WANDERING NATURE OF US GIRLS

Frankie McMillan

CANTERBURY UNIVERSITY PRESS

First published in 2022 by
CANTERBURY UNIVERSITY PRESS
University of Canterbury
Private Bag 4800, Christchurch
NEW ZEALAND

ISBN 978-1-98-850333-2

A catalogue record for this book is available from the National Library of New Zealand.

Editor: Emma Neale
Book design and layout: Aaron Beehre
Back cover: Washday at Moutere commune, early 1970s.
Half-title verso: The author in 1971. (Both photographs by Ron Hazlehurst)
Printed by Aaron Beehre, Ilam Press

Published with the support of Creative New Zealand

For Marvin,

who taught me how to wander.

Without you, I would never have gotten lost.

CONTENTS

THE UNDETECTABLE MYSTERY OF MY HUSBAND'S ILLNESS

WOMAN IN A BARREL

THE WANDERING NATURE OF US GIRLS

Magdalene, the sister we could not fathom

1.

My sister walked down the street carrying a fish so big you'd think she was more fish than girl and that huge fish was out to conquer the world, to bring men to their knees, women to reach for their knives and boys to whistle from the shadows. Everyone who saw my sister strolling down the street—puffing on a smoke, fish over her shoulder, fell silent as she passed. Which is just the way Magdalene liked it.

2.

My sister had a mouth like an overblown rose. Bad things fell from her tongue. But sometimes, hauling up the nets, Magdalene would sing, and her voice was so achingly beautiful you'd feel yourself slip, you'd feel the sweet tug of her all over again. Even the ship dog would sometimes stop howling for a few seconds, while her voice rose over the waves.

3.

Ask if my sister cursed the priest, stole other women's men and I'd have to say it was true, but ask if she could splint an albatross wing and send it back into the sky then that was also true. Do not ask about the missing dog.

4.

No one else on deck could wield a grappling hook like my sister. No one else but my sister could grow silence the way she could.

5.

Time passed. Magdalene began giving up things. She gave up the boats. She gave up smoking. She gave up the fishermen. One had thrown a knife at her, the blade had torn through her scalp. When she parted her hair, there was a lumpy ridge we were allowed to touch. It felt like the bony back of a fish.

6.

Magdalene, my sister, last seen swimming. On a wild stretch of the coast. In the sort of sea that spits out gravel. The sort of sea that sings up kelp, the sort of sea that pounds the shore, that roars and howls like a dog.

The wandering nature of us girls

1.

When we see the lake, when we see the strange blue
colour, and no ducks and no fishes, just clumps of reeds
at the side, when we sniff the air, we tell ourselves there
are dead men drowned in those waters and the lake is
a bad place but another day when us girls are bored of
whacking the stalks of foxgloves and bored of pulling live
cicadas off the mānuka to buzz in our fists, when we say,
'Let's go to the lake,' when we lose our way through the
mānuka and stumble down a rocky track and the rock
face still has got red ochre there, when we scrape the rock
with our fingernails, when we sniff, lick it to see if it smells
like paint, when a man comes up from the lake, his boots
sloshing with wet, when we press our backs to the rocks,
when he walks right past us, when we smell the dank lake
smell, the weedy smell of him, when he suddenly turns
to give us a terrible look, when we skedaddle back over
the rocky track, loose stuff coming down like sugar spill,
when we're back home is when we say: 'We saw a ghost, a
drowned man.' And then when everyone says there is no
lake, there has never been a lake, when we show them our
fingers smudged red, when our daddy shakes his head, says
we are crazy girls, when we swallow all our words about

the lake, so that later when a little boy goes missing, when night gathers and the men come over the paddock with torches, that is when everyone asks: '*Where is the lake, where is the lake, spit it out youse girls, we're talking about your lake.*'

2.

Because a little boy went missing, same day as we saw the man come up from the lake, we said he probably drowned the boy but because nothing bad ever happened in this town and because we were the sort of girls that people didn't think much of — because we played in the dump and came home limping on wooden crutches and didn't wash our hands — and because our hands were always grabbing things: the husks of cicadas, golden and crackly; the throats of medicine bottles; metal funnels and once a stethoscope from the dump that half worked — we lay down on the pine needle floor of our sanatorium and because it was the Chest ward we took turns squeezing each other's wrists, listening to each other's heartbeats, *ba boom, ba boom, ba boom* because that's how you could tell if a person was alive or dead, but if a person was in the water, you wouldn't know, you'd just see them go round and round like a water-logged cicada, their cries getting slowly weaker.

3.

Sometimes we dream of Mama; she swims through a mess of suitcases, bodies, holding presents aloft in her hands, but other times she is trapped in the train, her blurred face at the carriage window, fishes swimming past.

4.

When us girls play in the sanatorium dump, the dump of yellowish medicine bottles and cracked china pans, old canvas stretchers, and notebooks, all the notes about the patients, all the stuff about the TB and their blood and bones, when we feel sad in the dump, standing there in the sunlight, ankle-deep in paper, thinking how young and strong we are, when we look up at the sanatorium, the shining glass windows, where they park the sick outside in the blazing sun, when we see them, covering their heads with newspaper, us girls say we'll build a new sanatorium, with Baby Jesus's help we will mound up the pine needles, mound up four walls under the shady tree and we clap for the sanatorium, hands sticky with resin, we clap for our sanatorium that cures the sick, that has those folk rising to walk to the corner store for fizzy drink and smokes, and when we crouch down to make special cures, crushed leaves, dandelions, elderberries, and dregs drained from medicine bottles, so all the sick people can walk to the store, jingling their money in their dressing gown pockets, when we mix the potion, shake it up and hold the bottle to the light, when we sit inside our sanatorium, holding our bottles, hearing the magpies on the fence, when we say who will drink this potion, when we hear the McNelly kid, the one with the harelip, when we hear him, humming to himself as he climbs up the track, us girls look at each other with our knowing look, we look right into each other's eyes, the yellow glint of our eyes, our faces stretching a smile.

5.

'Chin up, girls,' they say, when our mama leaves on the train, 'Chin up,' we say to the kid, holding the medicine bottle to his lips, 'Chin up,' says our daddy, who forgets to bring groceries back home from the store, only sugar and tobacco, 'Chin up, head up,' we say to the boy as our hands settle on his shoulders and 'Chin up,' we whisper to the cicadas with torn off wings as we grasp their bodies, settle them under the mānuka trees and 'Chin up, youse girls,' they say after the terrible news Mama's train plunged off a bridge into the river, and 'Chin up,' we say again to the boy when we lead him outside our sanatorium and into the sun where he blinks nervously and we each take a hand and raise our faces to the warmth and wonder if it's worth doing a prayer and wonder if that might save us.

Swimming with Cliff

Cliff was the guy who sat in the upstairs glass booth at New World and read out the promotions over the intercom. '*Fresh, our cake is fresh! If you find fresher cake elsewhere, we'll give you your money back.*' Sometimes I'd just hang around the aisles with my trolley and laugh at the crummy things he said. Maybe he saw me laughing and thought I had a happy disposition and that's why he came down from his glass booth or maybe he saw me staring at the cake and thought I was too poor to buy cake but whatever, one thing led to another.

'Fancy a drive?' he said. He jerked his head towards the door. 'I'll take you up to see my hill-top paradise.'

~

'Uh, huh,' I said staring at the blow-up rubber pool, several fake palm trees and a recording system that blared out old Elvis songs.

'I know you don't get out much,' Cliff said waving his arm over his rubber pool. I tried to tell him I didn't get out much because of what travel was doing to the planet.

'Sure, sure,' he said.

'It's not a good day for me to swim,' I told him. 'I'll walk home now.'

~

The next time I went into the shop, Cliff began talking on the intercom about ending period poverty. '*Period poverty,*' Cliff's voice shrilled, '*and Tampax only a dollar a box!*' It made me feel uncomfortable, like maybe I'd left a spot of blood on the passenger seat of his car. I walked straight back home again. My mother took my side. 'He thinks he's king of the castle up in his glass booth,' she said. 'He doesn't even own that shop.'

~

Winter came early. People started boarding up their houses. My mother said Cliff was like his father, they let snow pile up on the roof. And their house was a clutter inside. Boxes of old grocery stock. Newspapers all over the floor. Stuff from garage sales: hand pumps, spares for inflating his rubber pool, old deck chairs, etcetera. 'Don't encourage him,' she said.

~

When I knocked on Cliff's door there was a lot of rustling of newspapers before he answered. He poked his head out. He was wearing a Hawaiian shirt covered with brightly coloured birds. There may have been a palm tree too but I didn't want to look.

My boots scuffed up the newspapers as I walked down

the hall behind him. ‘I’m not staying,’ I told him.

Up ahead the room was fiercely lit by a heat lamp. The walls glowed orange. I held out my arms to the warmth.

Cliff grinned. ‘You’ll be swimming, next,’ he said.

The winter swimming of my grandmother

People see my grandmother walk down the road with a towel over her shoulder. The local pig hunters, burly men in thick plaid jackets and fur-lined boots, shake their heads in disbelief. They think she's going for a *dip* somewhere. They imagine the brief frenzied plunge of an old woman.

'Don't tell them where I go,' she says.

My grandmother swims naked. She swims serious. She swims the lake, from the bank right over to the reeds on the other side, her pink woollen hat bobbing above the water. My aunty insists upon the hat. She's read up about hypothermia. 'I don't want to have to pull you dead from the water,' she says.

Ask my grandmother if she feels the cold and she laughs. She says the strange thing is that when she climbs out of the water her bare skin is flushed and tingly. As if she's been spanked.

She begins to stay in the water for longer.

Snow piles up on the woodshed roof. When my grandmother walks to the lake in her rubber boots she leaves behind a mushy trail of watery drift.

My aunt gets up before her, sneaks down to the water with a thermometer.

Who knows what will happen when the ice is too thick

to break. Who knows if the pig hunters silently watch
my grandmother swim, small brave animal that she is.
And who knows what makes the women in our family go
against the tide, strike out with such singular force.

Steadfast's breath

Some fellas go at a balloon as if getting a quick rise is some small triumph; others stretch the neck of the balloon out between their fingers and wink, as if they know things others don't; some seem reluctant to put their lips to rubber and only blow feeble spurts of breath into the balloon and you know, just know those fellas could never please a woman.

The Guinness record is 910 balloons per hour. But I don't expect to see that here. I had 100 in an hour and then the guy cramped up bad. Low on oxygen. Hands so clawed he could no longer tie off the balloon.

'Sit down, man,' I told him. 'No record is worth that.' This same long-haired fella comes back the next week with three women to cheer him on. The women dress exactly the same: all in blue with scarves around their heads.

He grins at them. Then his thin shoulders heave forward and back as he blows up the first balloon.

~

At 150 the stall is running out of space. The balloons bob around behind the counter, some sail off before I can catch them. The hot-dog man next door lets rip when one lands by his cooker. By then a crowd has formed, attracted by the commotion. The man gropes wildly around for the next balloon.

The three women yell his name. 'Steadfast! Steadfast!' I'm thinking Mormons. Serial wives. Then I'm wondering if there's something else going on here because this long-haired fella is a long way from beating any record. You don't know, none of us knows what goes on behind closed doors. When I give Steadfast a little stuffed toy for his efforts and watch who he gives it to — what sweet lady he favours — it's no surprise the whole crowd is watching with me.

~

The phone rings for the third time in a row. *Uh-oh*, I think, *what is it?* I've closed the stall for winter, just left the last of the red and yellow balloons bobbing in the front window.

A woman's voice on the phone tells me she needs me to open up the stall. Now. I can hear sobbing in the background. 'There's been a terrible accident,' she says. 'Please, can we have the balloons Steadfast blew up?'

~

The wives gather the balloons, and with arms full carry them to the back of an open boot. I don't ask any questions about the car accident: whether Steadfast is going to be buried with the balloons or whether they'll let them just drift off into the sky. Folks mourn in their own particular way. The youngest one hangs back. I find her behind the counter. She holds a red balloon over her head, air quietly hissing out. Her hair trembles. When his breath flows over her skin, she gives a little moan.

Stories told on the swings

Bobby's uncle sold rags and bones, not bones of the people who no longer needed their clothes but bones of dead cows: cows that got stuck in the swamp (with no tractor to pull them out) or cows that got bloated from eating the wrong sort of grass. You could pierce their swollen guts and such a terrible wind would come out you'd want to fold over and stop breathing but in the world there were even poorer people than Bobby's uncle and these people lived under bridges and if you gave them five dollars they would start humping each other. It was a noise like an animal pulling its leg out of the swamp, a sucky noise and sometimes the man on top would stop humping to light a cigarette, have a drag then go back to humping the woman again. After that story we swung our swings higher, riding the wind and not saying anything and later, much later, when I'd stopped leaving money under bridges and stopped drinking cow's milk, I sometimes went to the playground at night, sat on the swings and worked myself up into feeling sorry about the world, everything warming up, all the homeless people and then sorry about myself until I was so bloated by it all I had to get my pen knife, dig a little hole in my side and let the air come out.

Mr Whippy here and there, up the street, down the street, swerving his pink and cream van to avoid a dog, Mr Whippy, his face emperor white, hunched over the wheel wondering what dogs want with Mr Whippy.

Mr Whippy glancing in the rear vision mirror, kids still chasing him on bikes, their heads ducked under the handlebars, a mother jogging with a baby on her hip, *ice cream, ice cream* but Mr Whippy is wrecked, days spent leaning out his window, handing out cones with the perfect pointy top, pulling on levers, eyes squinting in the bright sun, his ears ringing.

Mr Whippy turning off his ice-cream shaped speakers because 'Green Sleeves' isn't what he wants to hear right now. He turns into a leafy suburb, checks in the mirror again, sighs with relief. Mr Whippy parks under a tree, eases himself into the back of the van, pours sacks of skim milk into the machine, fondly pats the metal side, restocks cones, wipes the sticky windowsill, tugs on his ear again.

Mrs Whippy shining a torch down his ear canal, 'Slush in his ear,' she laughs, 'a cul de sac of sprinkles,' and Mr Whippy, tired though he is, clamps a pale hand on her thigh. Mrs Whippy wriggles loose. Mr Whippy rises.

Out the bedroom door, down the hall, out into the

night. Mrs Whippy runs smooth and light as a girl and Mr Whippy follows, his legs pumping, dogs barking, the whole street cheering him on.

Romance in the lower and upper atmosphere

Him

Me with my girl in the grass gazing up at what looks like pinpricks in the great blanket of sky. It's getting cold. 'Well,' I say, 'have you had enough?'

Back inside, she goes around the house, lighting candles. I don't know what she's got against electricity. Swarms are drawn to the flame and there's an awful burning smell.

Later she tells me we're like identical stars but moving in opposite directions.

'That's just today,' I say, 'Just today you feel that way.'

That whole lunar month we orbit each other. My naked eye observes all her comings and goings, all her little divergences. She dyes her hair pink. She takes up running. Each day she runs farther and farther. When she gets up to speeds of 100km an hour I know I've got trouble. When a bright light streaks across the sky, followed by a trail of hot gas something inside me breaks.

I climb the roof. I square my jaw. 'Go on, shoot me,' I say, 'shoot me, lady star.'

Her

I don't go on about Pluto because lying beside me in the grass is my twin star who complains the grass is getting damp, it's the dew and, *have I had enough yet, have I had enough of being out here because inside could be a lot warmer* so we go inside and I light candles, white votive candles, one over there, one over there, until the whole house glows but I can see he's worried about swarms coming in and he looks at the open window as if by looking at it I'll know what he wants me to do and then he starts on about electricity, how it saves lives, and I tell him, 'It's not about saving anything,' but he keeps on about how we should support the electric companies, and he's like a dog with a bone, he won't let go until I'm forced to say that maybe he's right and he comes over and tells me I'm awfully pretty and he leans over and blows on my face and says his only wish is that we keep moving in the same direction and I can't help it but right there in the back of my mind, despite my love, the achy love I have for him that rises, tugs me into his gravitational field, despite all that, I see something sick and wounded I need to outrun.

When old fiddlers fall off their stools

You're watching a fly piggy-back another fly when your mama rushes to the window: she hears the fiddler playing and across the courtyard other mamas rush to their windows and they throw down pennies carefully wrapped in paper and the air is full of music and pennies raining down on the old fiddler and later when you whine you're never going to get new shoes and why does everyone wrap the pennies she looks at you sharply. 'Respect! They are artists, not beggars.' She gives you a shake and though you wriggle loose, pretend you don't know what she's talking about and say under your breath you're going to chuck dead flies down next time — when you hear the fiddler again, when the music soars into the street — you rush to the window, one fist full of pennies, the other softly tickling.

Explaining the *Sputnik* dog to my child

Possibly Laika stopped barking, stopped sending out signals to earth when the fan in the rocket broke, and possibly she dropped her head on her paws and dreamed of bones and dirt but possibly she saw the moon through the port hole, pricked up her ears, began to howl a Russian song.

possibly it was a race

Whatever else Laika was thinking as they strapped on her harness and whatever else they said except 'Please forgive us' and 'You have enough oxygen' and 'You're going round nine times, Laika, nine times, around the earth,' and whatever else happened, she kept sending the speed, the state of the weather, things flying past and whatever else she must have been restless, circling and circling and wearing the sky thin.

to send a man

Possibly Laika still runs through the skies and possibly the hunt for a small shaggy dog who can howl in C major has not come about and possibly, hey diddle diddle the cat and the fiddle and Laika is jumping

to the moon.

LAUGH, DOREEN

Laugh, Doreen

Because the Ferris wheel wouldn't start until all the seats were full, we called out to Doreen to come join us and she looked up from her candyfloss and came running all doggish and eager until we told her she had to sit in her own seat, because she could be radioactive because even though it was long ago her father had got an X-ray machine for his shoe shop: a black box you put your foot in and could see where the bone of your big toe met the tip of the shoe and your heel the back, the stories kept going round and round and each time we heard someone from our town had gotten cancer it was because they must have been to the shoe shop, even just walking past, the invisible rays could go right through you and when the Ferris wheel music finally started, the cogs and gears cranking and us swaying up to the very top, Doreen was always below, her eyes shut tight and then as we circled down we flung back our heads urging the Ferris wheel upward again.

'Laugh, Doreen,' we cried, 'laugh.'

And then for a brief time Doreen was up and we were down and she had a long-haired boyfriend who operated the go karts and she'd look at us as if she knew something we didn't and once her boyfriend came up behind her and put his long tattooed arms around her waist and Doreen laid her glowing face against his shoulder, but all the time looking at us in a funny sort of way. 'You don't know what you're missing,' she said and we felt the sort of emptiness where the big ride fills fast and we're left behind the fence with tired legs, clutching our tickets that shred to pieces in our hot sticky palms before our turn eventually comes round again.

Springing along in trick shoes

I wanted to wear those trick shoes, the ones the moonshiners wore, where the soles faced in the opposite direction so anyone looking for me would think I was coming towards them rather than away, and this meant I could stay hidden in the woods and think fugitive thoughts and maybe wash my feet in babbling brooks because they'd likely get stinky in those thick backward shoes. But my counsellor said, when I told her about the shoes, that I should try not to hide away from people and then I told her sometimes you have to throw Nazis off their tracks and she said, 'I hope you're using that term in a historical context,' so then I stopped talking about spies and shoes and when she asked me if I was still drinking I said it wasn't about the drinking, but I did feel as if I'd made a terrible mistake somewhere in my life, I'd wandered off the path and it was my hope that the trick shoes might lead me backwards to where I'd gone wrong, to where all this had started. I forgot to tell her the uplifting part: that the trick shoes were a yellow colour so if you walked through a field of daffodils you wouldn't know where your feet ended and the flowers began.

Wooden shoes

We ride our bikes around the neighbourhood hoping to see the man whose wife died, the man who wears wooden shoes, who can hardly speak English. Some days we think we will make his life better, we will stop and admire his windmill-shaped letter box, we will smile with our fresh, alive faces but other days we are convinced he is a spy from the war and we slip a note into his letter box, *we know what you did in the war*, then we race across the street to take it out again, to erase *in the war*, because it might be all the other things he did, *everybody does bad things* we say and then we watch to see if the man comes out to get the note but he just stands there in his bath robe, looking out of his big window so off we go wandering again and it's getting dark, dinner smells come wafting from the houses and, 'Are you tired?' we ask each other, 'Are your feet tired?' and if we both say yes at once, at exactly the same time, we will stop our wandering, we will go home and when the telephone rings with a terrible urgency — *they did what?* — we will be silent as trees, our feet dumb as blocks, leaves folding over our faces.

Walk, run

i

I don't know whose idea it was to kill the snails but we only did it because they were half dead anyway, crushed up in our pockets and what else could we do but put them out of their misery? We chucked them against the brick wall. Watched them froth up, make a silvery mess as they slid down. All except one that bounced off the wall and we had to kill it again. But just so nobody thinks we were bad, you have to know we dug graves for those snails. Scraped the dirt away with our hands. Piled moss in so they had a soft bed to lie on. We stuck a twig on the mound to mark the spot. Somebody said we should salute the dead snails so we did that too. It was getting dark, that sobby time when you want to fly flags or pray to Jesus but we ended up singing the National Anthem and that felt pretty good.

A group of snails is called a *walk*. But that's when they're alive.

ii

We run for Jesus. We run the streets, we run with our hands in our pockets, we run backwards squawking like chickens, we run, our faces stuffed with bread, we run past pigeons, daring them to snatch it from our mouths, we run like the Evangelists on wet Sundays, we run like playing cards falling from Joey Wheeler's hands, we run like he burned his smoke into our thighs, we run past the lake full of sunken bicycles, we run like old firemen startled from sleep by the ringing of bells, we run straight into church, bread dropping from our mouths. We stop running when we see Jesus. We stop to kiss his cold, marble feet.

The ring master's boys

Circus closed because the war was on but you wouldn't know it, we was all so alive on the inside, cartwheeling over the railway bridge and when the sleepers started shuddering under our feet we knowed it was the night trains coming, watched it sweep around the bend, horn blasting, lights flashing and us half blinded and jumping *now!* into the dark water below, bobbing up and down like candy apples, yelling out to each other, 'You there Sugar, you there, Mule, you there Joey boy?' and later slipping and clawing our way up the mud bank, running back to the bunkhouse through the forest, coming out taller than the trees, we were high flyers, we'd beat that train, we was magnificent and hurry now, wet clothes over the guy ropes, snatching a look at Joey boy, naked as a horse and already seeing the map of our own lives and not knowing if it was good or half good or otherwise but laughing anyway and later much later when we saw smoke and heard the guns we told ourselves we'd beat the train, and when the trees in the forest caught alight and the burning turned the sky red, we said we jumped the bridge and later again when black soot fell and our faces looked like cooked apples and we were hopping around in the heat we told ourselves, no matter, everyone gets saved in the circus.

The milk-bottle legs of the high-wire woman

1.

When I look at her legs I see upturned milk bottles, and I'm talking here of the glass bottles that milk used to come in and I love the shape of those legs, I could stay out all night on the frosty grass looking up at the wire and Miss Tatyana walking the wire so sweetly, only the guy ropes creaking and the twang of the metal pulley, and you know, those legs get my score, those legs belonging to Miss Tatyana all the way from Russia where they didn't have glass milk bottles, only Mr Stalin, his mouth a hard line, his eyebrows a nest of ideologies that to tell you the truth wouldn't suit a man like myself, a man who needs the freedom to pour his love into a vessel of his own choosing.

2.

They say anything you love, anything of value, is bound to make a break for freedom. Some nights I'm afraid I will lose Miss Tatyana. She'll move on from the wire. Trapeze, maybe. Or maybe it'll be the persuasion of a baby. In my dreams I throw her over my shoulder, gallop away with her on a horse. We get married in Porto, at night she wraps her milk-bottle legs around my throat. When I wake she's gone. My breath curdles into silence.

3.

I wait for Miss Tatyana by her caravan. Under a cool mackerel sky, only the fin of a moon peeking out. She moves between the tents and down the alleyway. I catch a glimpse of her legs as she walks past. And here's the thing. She knows I'm there waiting for her and she knows that I know she knows this and that's why I remain hidden in the grass. And she sits, smoking on the steps and I'm lying spread-eagled on my back, useless like something poured out. Smoke drifts over me, I close my eyes and I swallow and I swallow.

Jennie Worgan, the Midge's housewife

(Lilliputia, Coney Island, 1904)

The visitors like to observe
me shaking a red mat

from an upstairs window
or beating it over a barrel.

They like the live show
of small things done well.

This house is beyond gape
and gawk. This house has polished

floor boards, I wax on Tuesdays.
3 p.m. I serve high tea

to Princess Lottie and General Tot
in their drawing room. They are seen

discussing world affairs, the situation
in India. They drop crumbs,

I kick them under the carpet. When
the fire alarm goes off on the hour

and smoke fills the street
I run for the washing.

There is talk of a Ferris wheel
it paddles the air clean.

Once you sail to the top
below is never the same again.

Johnny Owl

'Watch yourself,' the boy is told and the boy must not trip over baby on the floor, must not give lip when no lip is needed and when he's sent to the big tent to help with the guy ropes, 'Watch yourself,' his mother says, 'don't go playing with the Lobster Boys,' and the boy thinks she doesn't have to tell him that, he's not going anywhere near those freak boys with their claw hands wanting to pinch at his thighs and he runs to the big top wondering how can you watch yourself if you are the one doing the watching of you watching yourself?

Where the trees stand at the back of the paddock is where he goes to try and figure things out. Like how to climb a tree in the dark and whether the tree is still a tree if no one can see it and, 'Watch yourself,' he says as his head smacks against the branch. 'Watch me!' he cries when he gets to the top, his palms sticky and sore. 'Watch me!'

Wonder is the time when the boy turns bigger, strutting in front of the fun house mirror. Hair in places he never had before and *watch yourself* comes back when the Lobster Boys peer down at him from the loft and when their voices thicken with longing for *what* the boy does not know but clasping is involved that's when the voice says, 'Watch what you say,' and then another voice shoves that to the side, it's his daddy's voice, come out of the ground, all earthy and woodsy, saying, 'A watched man never plays,' and the Lobster Boys scuttle around with that thought and then leave him alone.

Why his daddy died, is why his mother tells him to watch himself. A step gone wrong on the wire, and the show of his life is over. The boy swivels his neck from side to side. He can watch from here, there, over and away. Each day he twists his neck further and further until the burn sets in and the swivelling makes him dizzy.

Walk too close behind the grown boy and his head suddenly turns 180 and looks straight at you. Sometimes his eyes hold the shadows of trees, other times they bore right through you. After the evening show, he's the first to walk out of the tent, glass of beer in hand. He should really stay for the applause, he should really take off his bird suit but instead he sits on an upturned bucket in the dark thinking, *Lordy, this boy is someone to watch.*

Let us consider the blind

… whose hands wipe sunlight from the tree trunks, whose fingers read knot holes, whose thumbs are sticky with resin. They must rope themselves together on long walks lest they feel amorous and get lost in the moment.

Let us consider the babies of the blind. How their parents believe their round heads are mushrooms. How the wet nurse watches from the doorway. How she straddles the parents at night, shines a torch in their eyes to see if they are really blind and not just tricking.

What baby wants

We got him a rocking horse but our baby complained it was made of wood and it wasn't very nice for the tree, and we tried to explain how one thing always displaces another, but our baby was having none of it. He lay in my wife's arms, a tiny frown on his face.

A milky dribble ran from his mouth. 'You have to eat,' we said and eating means taking from others and we talked of all the different types of fruit; dark cherries falling in clusters, peaches raining down in a high wind, strawberries poking up from the earth. Our baby sighed, butted his little head into the breast.

When we offered him fruit, he threw it on the floor. Trampled it with his chubby feet. Red juice squeezed up between his toes. 'That's not very kind,' we told him. Our baby started laughing. His little chin wobbled. He shrieked with joy.

We put him outside under a tree. Birds made their nests in the high branches above. Our baby wrote a thesis on 'aerial domesticity'. We were amazed at the language he used. At night he slept under a pile of magnolia leaves. It was good to hear the faint rustling sound and know he was still alive. My wife stood by the window, hugging her full breasts in the moonlight.

The boy who grew antlers

It happened on the train, it happened between the south and the north, it happened among the throng of passengers, the yelling, the shoved suitcases, between dusk and dark, it happened so quickly — one, two, woody antlers growing from his head — and *careful* we cried as he tossed his magnificent antlers, and *careful* as they collided with the luggage rack and he bellowed with the joy of his new-found strength, his hooves clattered up and down the carriage and some passengers craned their necks to look for the guard, while others stared out into the inky night and we told ourselves *fine*, our son has turned into a stag, he clamours for his own path, *fine*, and then it happened the train sped into a tunnel and we feared he'd leap out, feared he'd break his neck, but then we heard his low breath in the dark, heard his antlers rutting against the metal berth and in the shadowy litter of the carriage, we filled our mouths with sweet smelling mint and murmured our gratitude that our son was okay, our son hadn't jumped, but when we heard the commotion, when we saw the passengers' suitcases hurtling past the window, when we saw flying scarves, hats and coats, when we saw the soldiers at the border with their guns, we raised our hands in the air, it was a stage, we explained, yes, just a stage our son was going through.

THE UNDETECTABLE MYSTERY OF MY HUSBAND'S ILLNESS

The undetectable mystery of my husband's illness

After my husband shakes the young oncologist's hand and says he hopes he has a marvellous career ahead of him, he's doing pretty well so far and after I tug him, laughing, down the long green corridor and out into the bright world, my husband punches his fist in the air and I say, 'Now everything will be all right, now you have a long life ahead of you,' and after we walk through the park kicking at the autumn leaves my husband grows quiet and I say, 'What?' and he turns to me with a long face and says, 'Hmm,' and I take his hand and say, 'Well then,' and he says, 'I expect so,' and I say, 'I think you're right,' and this goes on, our way of talking when we can't be bothered with real talking and then his fingers grip mine and he says, 'No party, I don't want a party,' and I say, 'Huh?' and he says, 'I'm not ready' and I say, 'Did you not hear what the doctor said?' and we stop and stare at a small boy in a red cap on his little trike and then we stare at the white geese on the lake, there's already too many and the males are fighting and fouling up the water and I drop his hand and say, 'Well?' and then he says, and his voice is full of the wonder of it, that he's lost his status, lost his status as a dying man and I try not to laugh but as we keep walking the path stretches longer and longer ahead and as dusk settles over the trees we walk faster, dark birds wheel overhead and still our home recedes farther and farther in the distance, not even a telescope could pick up the tiny dot.

Hawk-eyed girls

Us girls had eyes so sharp that from an upstairs window
we could see a snail's antlers emerge, we could see blades
of grass bow down, we could see the dumb fuck thrushes
pecking at the snail's shell, we could see that surrender
was not an option, we could see, even without turning
around, our mama in her swim suit, the way she threw
herself fearlessly into the ocean, the way she floated on her
back, not giving an inch to that water, not giving a tick for
the tides, not caring less about the currents and when she
came out glistening and risen and nothing like the other
mamas who sat under sun umbrellas, flicking their bright
orange toenails in the sand, we saw our mama was a wild
woman, and if we didn't keep an eye on her, every second
of the day and every second of the night, we might lose
her and that's why we leaned wide from the window, poked
out our heads, testing the night air, listening to the waves,
the rumbling drift wood, all the broken things that landed
on the shore.

Wishbone

My ex asked me to bring a dressed chicken and to keep it cool as it was a two-hour drive from my place to hers and 'Chubb,' she added, 'How have you been doing?' and I said, 'Not now, it's not a good time but I'll be there with the dressed chicken,' and all the while I was thinking it was so typical of her to say dressed chicken instead of stuffed chook, in the same way she now said inebriated instead of drunk, but I told her she should get the welcome mat out, I was driving to her place with the dressed chicken and it would be good to see the whānau for New Year's but as the time got nearer, as I pulled the cold chicken from the fridge, the idea of sitting down for a New Year's feed at the same table as that flight attendant she was screwing turned me right off so I had a few beers and after a bit the thought of driving to Nelson with a dressed chicken in the front of the ute had me laughing and I found some scissors and white paper and after a few attempts, I cut out a skirt and frilled the edges and all the way down the farm road and out onto the highway, the window wound down so the chicken would stay cool, I was thinking of my ex-wife's face when she saw the dressed chicken, but mostly I was wishing I'd put more Sellotape on the paper skirt because it really sucked, the way it was starting to unravel.

Armpits

Holly stands in the doorway; it is still dark but I know it is her, Holly from Hokitika, and something bad must have happened because she is just looking at us lying in bed and not able to say anything and I sit up and it must be the mother in me because I instinctively pull back the blankets and say, 'Climb in,' and Holly climbs in between us and then there are three of us and nobody is speaking, just looking at the big white rose plaster on the ceiling and then I say, 'Are you okay?' and Thom turns over, 'Are you okay?' and Holly, squashed in the middle, her bare legs pressed against mine says, 'Not really,' and I can feel Thom drawing in his breath and hoping nobody is suddenly going to declare their terrible love for each other the way it sometimes happens with flatmates and me thinking, *I hardly know her, I don't know what to say* and then after a bit Holly shifts, extends her arm behind my neck and she says she didn't know what else to do, and a fly buzzes lazily at the window, the sun just starting to come up and there's a smell of sweaty armpits, but not the overnight smell or the hot day smell of armpits but a fierce weaselly smell and I glance towards Holly's armpit, a dark cave, and then snatch my eyes away and say brightly, 'The sun is coming up,' but all the while I'm thinking Holly doesn't know she stinks or maybe she does but it's not important because something bad has happened and I say, mainly to the ceiling, 'Holly do you want to talk about it?' and Holly mumbles, 'It's all right,' and on the other side Thom shifts his legs politely and says, 'So you'd rather not talk about it,' and Holly says, 'No, but thank you and sorry,' and in the days that follow Holly never says what the terrible thing was that drove her from her bed to ours and I never say anything to Thom about her armpit smell because one day, I too might stumble from my bed in a strange city to stand in a doorway of people I hardly know, carrying some unspeakable grief inside me.

The uprising of my aunt

My aunt was always sweeping. She put her whole weight behind the broom like a man and that was my aunt. It was something and nothing to do with the dust. Then came the floods and she was the first to grab a yard broom, to sweep water from her living room, chase it, hollering into the street. And when the time came, she would not get into the boat, she held them off with her stiff broom and they would have taken her into the boat but she wouldn't have it and that was my aunt. And always she believed her luck would turn. She saw how messes could be cleaned up, how a street, a province, a country could come good again. She would not get into the boat, she wouldn't have it and she stayed in her home as the water rose as cardboard boxes, as mattresses and cats floated by. My aunt was always sweeping. That's how it was with my aunt. She was on the roof of her house with her pale straw broom. This was just before the house itself was swept away. She was waving the broom, my aunt was, she was waving the broom, she was sweeping the heavens clean.

We, the school dental nurses, 1960

We are the dental nurses, our cardigans tulip red, our feet rubber soled, we are the foot soldiers, we wave to the bomber jets as they unleash their arsenal of bright apples, oranges, bananas and bottles of milk, we applaud the attack on Bertie Germ, small grinning figure in his black racing car, for we are the defenders, the hole drillers, the saviour of the nation's teeth, beads of mercury roll in our palms, we pat the flushed faces of young boys, we say to the girls, 'Open wide and it'll soon be over,' we are the poster girls of health, we climb on chairs, dust off shelves, we steam and clean, we are the freshest of soldiers, if anyone harbours doubts, we hand them a cotton-wool fairy, if anyone screams our ears are thickly pale and silent, yes, we are the dental nurses, we march on the playground in our crisp white uniforms, our moon-round faces straight ahead as apples come raining down.

The elephant in the room

1.

My husband is a choker. Every now and again, he'll cough then suddenly rise, the dinner plate flung to the floor, food thrown everywhere. He runs outside, leans over the balcony. His body shudders as he tries to clear his airway. Sometimes he grasps an overhanging tree fern to steady himself.

We thought living at the edge of the bush might help his airways. We thought all that greenery would be good for him.

2.

He explains to visitors why he can't eat certain foods … the flap in his throat is faulty.

When I think of the throat I don't think of there being a flap in there. Or two passageways, one for food, one for air. The mechanisms of swallowing are a mystery to me. 'Can't you eat more slowly?' I say. 'Can't you count to ten before you swallow?'

One friend, who I suspect has a crush on him, always jumps up to offer water. Or rub his back in little circular motions. 'I hope you know the Heimlich manoeuvre,' she says.

It's hard to resume the conversation after a choking fit. Usually the conversation that follows is about his flap.

3.

I'm on my hands and knees, poking out a pea from under the leather sofa. My mind is not so much on the pea but the way a sofa seems to swallow objects. If I ever lose something, say my cell phone, it's bound to be wedged into the back. Under the sofa it smells like elephant. I've never smelt an elephant up close but I think, *this is how it would smell.* This is the sort of thing I find interesting but it doesn't seem to go anywhere in a conversation.

4.

My husband lurches inside. 'Heimlich,' he gasps. He points dumbly to his back.

He's never asked for this before.

I jump up. I put my arms around his middle, my fingers search blindly for the bony ridge … the diaphragm. But he is a big man and my arms scarcely go around him. We stagger around the floor, my face pressed to his warm back.

In desperation I hit him. I pound his back. My hands, my fists raining down on his sweat-soaked shirt.

We haven't made love for years. Now we are involved in a terrible struggle.

5.

Outside, wind ploughs through the flaxes, the tree ferns wave and as we lie there in a sweet tangle I imagine he is thinking of the latest story he will tell about his flap. But instead he turns to me, 'We are so lucky,' he says, 'so very, very lucky.'

Unripe fruit

Nobody else grew strawberries like hers, your mother said, some grew strawberries but they were mean things with heavily pitted flesh and hers were big and sweet and evenly coloured and she used real straw as bedding, not mulched newspaper or dirty looking sawdust that attracted the slugs and you told your mother you'd always grow strawberries her way, you'd do the runners right, you'd keep them away from the birds, the pests and you'd *never* pick them early and then one morning your mother raised herself from the bed and told you to get the bucket and you wondered why she wasn't up picking the strawberries herself but she said she had a little stomach ache and that Eddie was coming over soon so you should stay out of his way and see how many ripe strawberries you could pick but when you were squatting there, running your hands through the silken straw, fingers searching for the best red ones that often lay hidden, winking like a big fat ruby, you heard her moaning and you rushed inside and Eddie was already there in the doorway saying, 'Has it come away, honey?' and you stared at your mother lying there so pale in the bed, sheets all tossed and she manages a cheery little wave, and you say, 'Shall I ring someone?' and '*No!*' they both cry, and then Eddie steps outside, cupping his hands around a smoke, looking towards the road and you go back to the strawberries, your mother still moaning, and every time you run into the house you're sent back outside again and then you fall on your knees you rip out a handful of pale strawberries, still hard and unformed and you throw them against the fence, *ping, ping,* and that's how Eddie finds you, your hands full of unripe berries, leaves scattered and the bucket tipped over.

The girl from the laundromat

You remember when he said you were beautiful, a clean thing that would save him. You were both running towards the Alligator Aquarium on the waterfront. There was a small open shaft on the roof, he said, easy to slip through. He wanted to show you the alligators, boy, they could move he said, those alligators could move if you threw them something.

You remember the tight squeeze through the dirty shaft. 'You go, you beautiful thing,' he said and that made you forget you were just a skinny girl who slept in the back of the laundromat, made you forget the smell of dirty clothes and unwashed dreams.

Watching the alligators, the way they thrashed their tails, the brackish water spraying over the side, set your heart beating. He pulled you away from the tank. You thought it would be cool to make out with him, right there on the swampy floor with the restless alligators urging you on. You thought no other girl would do that with him.

You turned to face him, to offer him your beautiful, clean lips but he was already in the office. You heard the till open, the rattle of coins.

He hadn't yet told you to run for your life. You hadn't yet taken off your red halter top, stood on tippy toes, waving it at the alligators.

Yah, yah, if the wind changes, your face will stick

When the wind blows I shut my eyes, that way I can hear
how fast it's coming, can hear the leaves stir, the sparrows
in our trees trying to shush things up, the bit of tin on the
shed roof rattle and when the wind gets close I run to the
mirror in the wash house, only the glass is a bit cracked so I
angle my head to the side then I smile, my best pouty smile
and outside I hear that flighty wind roughing up the firs, a
bucket roll over the yard, a window slam, and back in the
mirror I gasp, *my mouth has turned into a beak.* I give my head
a little punch but that doesn't change anything, and now
my shoulder blades twitch so I rip off my blouse to check
and then I don't know why but I take off my pants as well
and stand there naked, trying to figure out how to get all of
me now in the cracked mirror, all of me smiling, bobbing
up and down, hopping around in the bird house but then
a gust blows the wash house door wide open, the wind
catches my startled face and that's how Mama finds me, she
shakes her head, 'Where did I go wrong?' she begins.

The movie of your life

Your sister grew wild, nobody could catch her. She's *acting out* the neighbours said. You had to bike after her, to try and bring her home. But home was not like the Disney movies, home was half-starved cats that wanted to leap into the fridge every time the door was opened. 'I'll escape with you,' you told her. You were yelling this as she ran down the street. You were yelling this as her boyfriend's Chevy pulled up beside her. The neighbours hung over the fence to watch. You were clawing your sister. She was pushing you off. Those girls are *making a scene,* the neighbours said.

Hunting my father's voice, County Down

It begins with the medieval
throat clearing of crows

high over Scrabo tower. You
were the boy your mother

forgot to drown and still
you holler for help

So here's a bloody conundrum
shot to blazes and back

and your brother Jimmy
in a slow swim to save you

Dad, the land is full of boulders
an apron of stones

to feed a nanny goat
chalk a plenty to soften your voice

All those stories, enough
to hang a man, come Easter

All that dreaming
the time it took

to dig breath for the fire
the knot and bog

of the back parlour where Jimmy
washed roosters

and sister Maureen, her hair
lovely enough to stop your throat

The laughing epidemic

The monkey started it all, flashing its red bottom among the trees, making the schoolgirls helpless with laughter, making them cover their faces with their books, but still the laughter grew. The laughter grew, it swelled, into loud guffaws, it reached the teacher's ears, she stood by the blackboard, chalk in hand, stood ready to throw the chalk at the laughing girls. The laughing girls pulled on each other's braids, they staggered to their feet, tears streaming down their faces and despite herself the teacher couldn't help but grin, *crazy girls,* and she kept on grinning and then she began to laugh, she threw back her head and rocked with laughter and at the sight of their teacher now gasping, holding her belly, twisting the folds of her cotton frock, the other students began to join in, because *their teacher, their teacher* was laughing. Was laughing!

The wild noise spread to the next classroom, the laugh snowballed, it went barrelling down the hallway, rolled under the door of Miss Emecheta's room. Rolled under the door of Miss Emecheta's room was a laugh so infectious, she began to snort and splutter but fearing her weak bladder, she crossed her legs and stuffed her hand in her mouth. Stuffed her hand in her mouth and stared sternly at her students as if the noise was temporary, as if the laugh would soon subside. *As if the laugh would soon subside* was hopeful thinking. The bigger girls screamed with laughter, they knew exactly why their teacher had crossed her legs, and the laughter grew even bigger until footsteps were heard running from the office and there was the headmistress.

There was the headmistress, opening the door to the raucous sound of laughter that swirled through the room to fly through the open windows, right over the whole school, that deafening sound of mirth; pealing, shrieking, spluttering, and the headmistress powerless in its wake, joined in the laughter, helpless and startled as anyone she lay in the heat on the wooden floor beside Miss Emecheta — the junior teacher she'd once disliked, but now was feeling rather fond of. Rather fond for a fellow sufferer, the headmistress lay on the floor, shaking with laughter as a movement ran through the trees, a shiver of leaves, the dart of a monkey.

Cuba and other stand-offs

One summer, to please my brother I brought him home a girl. The girl's name was Natashya; she had dark, very short hair and a fine moustache on her upper lip. She'd moved into our street after being adopted by the McAllisters — even though she was twelve and not much adoption left in her. I'd pumped her up with stories of my handsome brother.

Natashya did her hair in the mirror and put on a tight white blouse. I knew my brother would be pleased with her big breasts. She wasn't very pretty but I knew enough about boys that they liked breasts and hips and girls who flared their nostrils and said they were up for anything. And on the long walk back to my house I learnt some more things. Natashya said she'd once been in a home for bad girls. Some of the bigger girls there would go on heat, just like cows. They'd look all swollen and bloated and move slowly and said they felt achy down there. Natashya stopped under a tree. Waved her blouse out in front of her. 'Aren't you hot?' she said.

Most of the neighbours were inside, their blinds pulled down against the heat. I pointed out the red roof of our house, told her my brother would be waiting. I thought of how cheered up he'd be to see a girl other than his sister.

He'd stop listening to his transistor radio about the terrible news in Cuba.

We rested a bit in the shade. I thought of telling her what my brother had said. Khrushchev was going to blow up the world. But Natashya was busy ripping up grass. Drying her sweaty underarms with the feathery tufts.

'You can put your head under the hose when we get there,' I told her. 'That will cool you off.'

Natashya stood up. I could sense she was about to bolt; to run back to the McAllister's place. Later she would, after giving my brother a black eye, but now she stood there, her mouth working up and down, a sorrowful look in her eye.

'I'm used to swimming pools,' she said. 'And cars. I'm not used to all this walking.'

I stared at her flushed face. It was a tense moment. Anybody looking down would have seen us squaring off, shading our eyes against the too bright sun.

Centaur Man — Centaur Woman

(after Redon)

They must have come during the night
wandered into my yard

they look well fed their rumps
lardy with sweet grass

sprung from Mount Pelion

She holds hands with him
but her gaze is elsewhere

saddled with some small grief

these two don't shudder
and shake like Greek gods

don't appear to be drunk
or hell bent on drumming

their hooves against my door
maybe the male is Chiron

and the sad look on her face

is because she's fetched up in this place

and it should be snowing
but it isn't

I tell my daughters
slice apples

dip in frosted sugar
wrap each in a cabbage leaf

before throwing them down
to the frosty yard —

where they shyly stand
in the first patch of sunlight

Horse love

If someone saves you, you're either mad at them or love them forever and it was that way with me and Hine. It wasn't the usual sort of love. Or the usual sort of save. She doesn't pull me clear from a runaway horse, drag me out from under its belly, the sharp hooves flailing the air. What she does is walk into our living room, hands on hips, eyeball my nervous uncle — who isn't even my real uncle — and say, 'Lonnie's not going driving with you anymore.' My uncle just about chokes on his cake. He can see Hine is the sort of girl who could say anything. He doesn't yet know what she knows, whether she might be the canary about to sing, to put an end to the Saturday driving lessons down lonely roads, *girl, keep your eyes on the road, watch that nasty bend*, while the car starts and shudders and picks up speed through a corridor of trees.

He calls it a 'meander.' 'I'll take the girl for a meander,' he calls to my mother, head out the window of his Chev. My mother is a tamed thrush. She cocks her head, coos, 'That would be lovely, Rex.' She tells me I'm lucky to get free driving lessons and not to give him any trouble.

Hine pushes me towards the door. 'Go,' she laughs. Down at the paddock we practise being horses, shaking our manes, running wild. Then we turn, approach slowly, ever so slowly until our noses touch. Our nostrils flicker, our rubbery lips pucker. Hine's breath is warm on my cheek. She'll either bite me or kiss me, I never know which. Later she'll say this is another one of my made-up stories about her.

Seeing Stan

(sequel to 'Truthful Lies')

Twenty years later, I saw Stan again. 'You've got a nerve,' he said. It was outside the court house and Stan was holding a briefcase and his hair, that dark hair of his, still bolting upright from his head. 'You've got a nerve,' he said, 'showing up like this,' and I stood there and I might have said, 'Just a minute …' and he might have said, looking at his watch, 'One fuckin' minute,' and we might have gone to the café over the road to where all the crim lawyers hung out, with their shiny shoes and subpoenas and bold voices and I might have watched Stan do a bit of a jump to get seated or I might have looked away. But I did go to the counter, and I did come back with two hot waters and two slices of ginger crunch and Stan might have raised his eyebrows at the hot water, the hot water that was all we could afford in the Poor days and I might have said, 'So that's all changed too?' and he might have said he's earning a whack now and I might have thought of the word 'whack' and how, when we lived in the garage, he'd cheerfully whack his penis against my leg on his way outside for a leak and I might have said, 'Good for you,' and he might have sighed and looked at me, looked at me hard and I might have thought, has he picked up on that thought, that thought of him casually whacking his penis on my bare leg as he passed, because lately I can think a thing and next moment that thought is in someone else's head and they're saying just what I was thinking ... and then Stan began patting my hand, like it was some friendly animal and it was at that moment I asked Stan — in the crowded café — it was at that moment I asked him, 'What happened to our son?'

Can you believe what people say?

You should hear people in court. They tell the most awful lies. Sometimes I'd sit in the back of the court, because no one minds if you sit there quietly and I'd just watch, hoping I'd see Stan but I could never work out the days he was there, so instead I watched the people being questioned in the witness stand. *That's a lie*, I'd say to myself. *That's a fuckin' lie.*

MADAME YETI

Madame Yeti

There was a man she used to see, but only on Tuesdays. He sold refrigerators from the back of a warehouse, a warehouse so cold she named it the Tundra. There was a heater and sometimes — afterwards — they'd huddle around the glowing bars in the gloom of the building. 'What more could you want?' he'd say, stretching his bare arms out to the warmth.

She called him the Woolly Mammoth. Because of his chest hair and the thick pelt that grew over his shoulder blades. 'What exactly,' she said, happily tugging at the hair, 'is the point of that?'

He called her Madame Yeti. Because of her long skirts, her big heavy feet. But more because her eyes always seemed to be on the edge of things.

After a while Tuesdays were never enough. She began walking by on Thursdays. There, by the warehouse door, she'd casually stop. Pretend to fetch a stone up from her fur-lined boot. It was dark back there, in the Tundra. She didn't know what was back there on those other days. Sometimes, leaning in, she thought she heard animal sounds and she imagined arctic hares bounding over the stacked refrigerators, musk-ox scratching their heavy sides against the appliances. Once she heard him on the phone to a customer. He was saying what to look for in a fridge. 'A freezer on the bottom is better than a freezer on the top,' he said.

Sundays came and went. Madame Yeti had her own spiritual beliefs. She visited her parents' graves, took long-stemmed lilies and little offerings of food. 'I didn't know what it was to be old,' she said, and 'I'm sorry.'

Mondays were better days. Only one more day before she could see him again. She washed her hair, wove the long plaits around her head. She inspected her nails, her feet, looked inside her mouth and with the edge of a spoon, scraped her tongue clean.

On Tuesdays she tried not to be too eager. She slowed her pace. Tugged at the strings of her fur-lined hood. At the door she paused. Through the mist at the back of the warehouse, the Woolly Mammoth dipped his massive head. His tusks, scooped the air, made her giddy with longing. She had a Neanderthal thought. There were no days in the week. This meant she could lie, rocked in the curve of his tusks, in an endless winter.

Our uncles, us girls

The uncles come in from the cold
lay their rifles on the kitchen table.

It is Saturday night. Snow falls —

the nudging drift of horses before they break
into a canter. Snow falls —

our mother throws a sheet into the air. Snow falls —
the war beckons through the window.

When snow doesn't fall the uncles
bring out their accordions,

they stamp their feet, they roar with laughter
slam good-natured bodies together.

Later they lie still

as dead horses on the living room floor,
numb to our ministrations.

We straighten limbs, lay our ears to their chests,
listen for their heartbeats.

Snow falls, we run like soldiers when they stir.

What extremely muscular horses can teach us about climate change

She tells me she's read about it, this link between horses and climate change, but when she went to the internet a message popped up *page not found* and all she can imagine is that the horse's breath is a ferocious wind that lays the desert or the tundra or whatever to waste and, really her mind is saddled up with the strangest of facts; how an octopus has three hearts, how bees sleep in pairs and hug each other's knees at night and, 'Stop right there,' I tell her because I know what's coming next, it will be about the gorillas making a new nest each night in the trees, and the male sleeping below to ward off hyenas or other dangerous beasts and she lies on the double bed in the motel room, far, far away from the desert or tundra or jungle or savannah, and she points to the single bed by the door and tells me if I were the male gorilla I'd be sleeping right there, ready to defend the troop and I shake my head *troop?* but she's read about it, it's the collective noun, so then I take off my belt and trousers, and I ask her if I'm not an extremely muscular fella and '*Page not found*,' she says, '*page not found.*'

Branching out

1.

We watch Papa watching Mama get dressed in front of the mirror. Papa comes up behind, a strange look in his eye and he puts his arms around her and then there are the two of them looking at themselves in the oval mirror and he says, 'You don't have to go,' and she says, 'Yes I have to go.' Then he strokes her thick brown hair and sighs and says 'Do you need help starting the car?' and Mama says she can crank that old Ford up in no time and now could everyone get out of the room please because she has to get ready.

Papa looks at us, standing in the doorway. He flexes his arm muscles.'Who's the strongest man in the world?' he says.

Papa walks around the kitchen then heads for the woodshed. We hear the thwack, thwack of the axe splitting wood and then he's back inside again talking about the wood supply and Mama says he could always grow more trees and he says, 'Good idea, keep talking,' but Mama isn't really wanting to talk, she's wanting to get out the house, all dressed up and that's when Papa grabs her. She laughs and Papa laughs hauling up her blouse and now he's got a felt tip pen in his hand and he's writing something over her pale belly and we crowd around to see the wobbly writing, the big arrow pointing down her underpants. **Keep out of here.** And Mama says, 'Are you done, you crazy fool?' and she rushes to the bathroom and slams the door shut.

And Papa looks pleased and says he's made a stand but whether he's talking of trees or Mama's boyfriend we don't know but slink low behind the couch because we do know this thing hasn't finished yet, this thing could branch out wide and overtake the house and bring us all crashing down.

2.

The man Mama loves pitches his tent in our paddock and that's the first mistake Papa says, that pool of water nearby is full of mosquitos and we watch the man build a little fire outside, snapping branches over his knee, and crouching down low, to blow on the flame and then jumping up to slap at the mosquitos and us kids laughing because why would Mama want a fire outside when Papa's got the range on, fresh herrings in the pan, sizzling with butter, so we keep watching and no surprise when the man comes up to the house needing more matches and no surprise when Papa says, 'For God's sake, man, come up here for dinner,' and Mama trying to keep a straight face and later when the man helps dry the dishes and Papa stares out the window above the sink, when he turns to Mama and says, 'Can I ask where you're sleeping tonight?' and we stare at each other, we stare at the man twisting the striped tea towel around and around his hand, we stare at Mama who's staring at Papa and nobody speaks until Papa says in a small voice, 'I thought so.'

And the second mistake, Papa says, standing on the veranda looking down at the glow in the paddock, is that some silly bugger hasn't stamped out the fire. And us kids shake our heads when Papa says, 'You wouldn't be stupid buggers like that, would you, you wouldn't leave a fire untended like that?' and 'No,' we chorus, 'we wouldn't do that.' So then Papa pulls on his boots and we watch him go into the shed, a gun, a spade? over his shoulder and though he's told us we have to stay inside, there'll be nets to pull in in the morning, we follow him through the trees to the paddock, his lantern lighting up the trunks and us careful not to scutter a branch or bump into each other and then up ahead we hear Mama's surprised cry and we hurry on and there's Papa hauling the man out of the tent and in the firelight we see he's naked, trying to cover his stiffy and Papa grabs his spade and that's when us kids start screaming and that's when Papa scoops up some dirt, stands there blinking, the full spade wobbling and no one knowing where that dirt is heading.

Not the target

Walking through trees and a friend texts *are you okay* and I wonder why I wouldn't be okay and then another text and there's five dead and a gunman on the loose and I quicken my pace and another text comes in, terrorists and twenty-seven dead and meanwhile my granddaughter hears gun shots from the mosque down the road and the teacher closes the curtains and her friends huddle in the corner, flicking through their cell phones to find the gun man's video, live streaming and not knowing if it's a game or for real while across town another granddaughter hurries home from the climate change protest and in the days that follow I keep watch over my granddaughters: one has changed her hairstyle, the other has taken to climbing trees, she's fashioned a bow and arrow from bamboo, she climbs to the highest branch and sits there quietly, the bow across her knee, birds flying overhead.

Displaced things

We started to kiss each other goodbye like old people. We started saying things like, 'You take care, watch the traffic, watch out for marauding beasts, men wielding guns.' You started asking what time I'd be home and what vegetables did I want for dinner. We stayed up late worrying about caged animals. We fell down. We tried to lift ourselves up by wearing T-shirts saying I AM VEGAN. We were not whakamā about letting everyone know what everyone else already knew. Everywhere we went we displaced things, our feet disturbed insects, grass, our heads occupied the air. When areoplanes flew across the sky we waited underneath, watched scraps of paper fall; pamphlets advising, *Surrender.*

Some things you fell

Other men brought me trouble but Leo brought me trailer loads of wood. It was a cold winter and I needed to keep the wood range on, or the water pipes would freeze. We sat side by side with our feet in the oven. When he told me I was the third most beautiful woman in the South Island, I opened up the fire box to let the heat out. When I told him he was the fourth most intelligent man in Aotearoa, he laughed, plonked his heavy-socked feet over mine. These were the fun times, jabbing at words, the soft underbelly of them.

When it got really cold we'd haul the tin bath in front of the fire. Sit in the steaming heat, our knees hunched up under our chins. I'd grope between his legs, cup his soft dick in my hands. Marvel at how easily the thing floated. Or that's the way I remember it.

One night Leo's wife came to my door. She looked like an elderly girl with her long hair and her arms folded over her thin chest. 'You know he's dying?' she said.

He laughed when I told him that. He heaved a wheelbarrow of pine into the shed. 'She would say that.' I thought about his wife for a bit, the many ways in which she must have loved him.

Then I walked inside, looked for Leo's jacket. *A card inside with a doctor's appointment?* I scrolled through his phone

… *maybe a reminder message?* Outside came the dull thud of the axe splitting the wood. I stared out the window. Shivered at the thought of all the trees that had to be felled, just to keep us warm.

Coming towards her, a thoroughly decent man off Bumble

She thought if they met, something terrible would cross her face, some arctic flare in her eye, some shy marking that would show just what kind of species she was. She wanted to scuttle down between a cleft in the rocks, haul strands of kelp over the entrance. She'd rather have salt-ridden driftwood under her thighs, hard slab of rock overhead than have to meet his eye. When he ambled past, cheerfully whistling, she shrank down further into the driftwood. When her face began to burn with shame and her coat began to smoulder, she feared she would burn in her own nest. Already the marram grass was waving as if to catch his attention. Already, the gulls were screaming like jilted lovers.

The existential crab colony of Kyushu Bay

so frugal we sleep on sand
under an upturned dinghy

my lover clasps me tight
for thirty days and nights

I dream of shipwrecks, the light-
house keeper who feeds me

gastropods, morsels of seaweed
until my belly begins to swell

and I'm back in the house market
for something larger. meanwhile

the paddle crabs play music
how can I explain this to myself?

I see them scoop salty water
blow through their gill chambers

such a riot it gets
the hermits out of hiding

this is the nature of serendipity
I follow their grey scuttle

their Japanese bustle and go
as they check out the vacancies

of mollusc and carapace. *such*
longing to find a place to call home

to say this is mine to the edge of my shell
and over there stranger is you

my lover says we are all renters —
none of us know the landlord

WOMAN IN A BARREL

Seven starts to the tumbling of Annie Edson

(Niagara Falls, 1901)

1.

Picture the cold dark inside of the barrel. Annie feeling her way over the padded mattress to a harness hanging from the side. The barrel sways in the water. Picture her fastening herself upright into the harness, pulling the leather strap tight across her chest. Picture Annie flailing about, she can't find her lucky heart-shaped pillow. Now picture the barrel picking up speed, with the current, heading straight towards the falls.

2.

It's not as if falling was something new. Early on, I fell from my crib, I fell through haystacks, I fell from grace, I fell behind the church to kiss the bridesmaids, I fell between heaven and hell then into marriage and when my good husband was taken off to war I fell into despair. When cholera came and took the baby I fell so low I did not know I'd fallen. I fell short of loving men. I fell into debt. I fell about the house; birds beat against the windows, mould grew upon the cheese, yet in the dark I dreamed that fame could come with falling.

3.

Us boatmen watch the wind fall. Then we anchor by Goat Island so we can get Mrs Taylor and the barrel ready without too much sway. When she begins undressing, we turn our backs. Let the oars rest in the locks, listen to the falls. We'd done talking. We'd told her *no one* has ever survived going over in a barrel, it was madness it was. She was killing herself and on her *birthday*.

We turn around. She stands there, a man's coat flung over her shoulders. A big flowery hat on her head. Can't help but stare. The long barrel begins bobbing alongside the boat. Later it'll have white letters painted on it. *Heroine of Niagara Falls*. But we don't know that now.

We spit on our thumbs, hold them up to see which way the wind's coming.

4.

If I hide my grey hair under a hat, if I lie about my age, I have my good reasons.

5.

My poor head is full of measurements. The length of the barrel staves, the circumference of the iron hoops, the position of the bung hole, the exact weight of the anvil at the bottom so the barrel floats upright during the ride. I look the barrel maker in the eye. I tell him I have every expectation of surviving.

Night comes. I talk to my lucky heart-shaped pillow, I talk about the barrel maker, the boatmen, the beef-faced newspaper men, I talk about their buffoonery, their banter and blather, I talk about the Buffalo Exposition, the crowds that await me, how lucky the timing was for my stunt, and I go on talking while candle light gives such a ruby glow to the pillow I push my cheek into the plump mounds of silk and *Maude, Maude, Maude* I breathe, though I don't know any Maude, not even a bridesmaid Maude and later, to knock some sense into my God-fearing self, I draw my knees up to my chin, listen to the noise of the falls and '*Brace, brace, brace!*' I cry.

6.

A huge crowd had gathered on the Goat Island bank. Some had been there the previous day when the wind got too fierce to get the barrel out. Over the noise of the falls we hear snatches of a voice shouting from the wharf. '*Mrs Taylor, refined teacher of New York … What are the bets … Will she take the plunge?*' We head around the inlet into view. The crowd erupts in cheers. Horns blast the air. We pause a bit as Mrs Taylor stands in the boat, big hat on her head, her arms held out to the falls.

7.

Born I was in 1804 though for my own purposes I say the date was 1824 and if anyone looks askance at my grey hair

I say, 'What else do you expect having been widowed and lost a child in the same year?' and after a while I repeat 'I'm forty-three' so often I start to believe it and I'm so nicely harnessed in to my younger self I think there's no pickle I can't get out of and that leads me to daredevil thoughts and that leads to the barrel and going over the Niagara Falls.

Bring me a heart-shaped pillow, bring an anvil so the barrel stays upright, bring a bicycle pump to push more air inside, bring a cork or two for emergency holes, bring a feathered mattress, bring a stout rope to tow the barrel behind the boat, bring a boy or two to cut the rope and send me adrift.

Black cape-jacket off, my bonnet, my outer garments rolled into a ball and Lord, how tender I feel towards my clothes as I hand them over for safe keeping.

Barrel so dark, and my knees hunched up over my chest and *hello* says the lucky heart-shaped pillow and 'Farewell!' shout the boys standing in the boat.

Bejesus … bejesus … wwhhaa … oh … mother … of saaavemeee … the waer … waer … didna guess … blasenouta cannonbe eeeasier … be jeesus — all quiet … here comes the plunge …

'Bet you a thousand to one, she didn't survive,' they say even as they're sawing the top of the barrel open, even as I stagger out and have the wits to curtsey and all night the doctors stay with me as I sleep, as I fall into darkness, as

I whisper 'Happy Birthday' to myself, as I say 'Queen of the Mist,' as I say, 'Heroine of Niagara Falls,' as I say it so often I go under knowing it to be true.

A litany of the washing machines in my life

<u>*Simpson*</u>. Mama doesn't eat for a week so she can pay off the new washing machine. She feeds the wet clothes through the wringer. They go through the rollers, fat and sudsy, come out flat to land in a concrete tub of water. I hardly know this skinny new Mama standing in high heels in charge of a washing machine.

<u>*Champion. Christchurch*</u>. The lever on the side doesn't work. My sister gives the washing machine a kick. 'Bingo!' cries the baby. She stands on a chair, watching the clothes go round and round. When her arm gets caught in the wringer the rubber rollers pull her in right up to her neck. I run to the neighbours for help. 'Is your mother out again?' Mrs Flynn says.

<u>*Beattie. With spin dry*</u>. Student flat. The machine shudders violently in the downstairs room. It has never been the same since the fire. The floor pools with stagnant water; the risk of electrocution. I ring Mama. 'Wear rubber-soled shoes when you do the washing,' she says. 'Promise me you'll always wear rubber soles.'

<u>*Bath. Enamel*</u>. My boyfriend sings in the bath, wet clothes draped over his legs. 'We come on the sloop John B. my grandfather and me, around Nassau town we did roam …' When he's finished scrubbing he opens the window. Hurls

the sudsy clothes out onto the lawn. Later he'll appear around the side of the house, carrying a hose. Much later he'll get drunk and pass out in the bath.

Arms that are also washing machines. We live in a plywood hut surrounded by scrubby bush. There is no power and for a while, no running water. My sister and I use the river, squatting on the stones, soap slipping, the toddler's nappies blooming white in the rushing water. While we laugh, the weka steal our soap.

Kent Worthington. Motueka. The washing machine stands in a small store room behind the kitchen. A wicker bassinette sits on the bench. The machine slaps back and forth. On top of the clothes is a rat. Round and round sails the small animal on its hind legs. No one knows what to do. (I can't kill a rat because I'm pregnant.)

Copper boiler. The Moutere commune overlooks the paddock. A copper boiler with fire grate below. Two rough concrete tubs beside it, one mounted with a hand wringer. There is a long stick. I stir the boiling water, the drenched tangle of clothes. I look out over the paddock. There will be no baby clothes in this load.

Out-sourced laundry. Sydney hospice. The first AIDS patients arrive. At first no one knows for sure how the disease is spread. I am dressed in a gown, plastic apron, mask and white gumboots. I strip the bed, put the dirty linen in blue bags. The man, sitting patiently in his pyjamas, asks for a doctor. 'They are not on site,' I have to tell him. *Like the laundry*, I want to say, but don't.

The bike-powered washing machine. A pulley system is attached to the back wheel of a mounted bicycle. I grate Sunlight soap into the washing machine bowl. Then I pedal hard and the agitator in the washing machine moves sluggishly, back and forth, back and forth. When I have been biking for five minutes I ring the bell. Johnny comes out, hands me the new baby, takes his turn on the bike. We have not yet quarrelled. He has not yet fallen in love with someone else. I have not yet tied him to the bike-powered washing machine, told him he cannot leave.

The bike-powered washing machine with more comfortable seat. 'This is daft,' Mama says. 'Just daft.' When no one is looking she climbs up on the bike, does a pedal or two then gets down again.

Beattie, powered by generator. A Briggs & Stratton motor. The heavy beat of the generator reverberates through the bush. Swarms of excited cicadas fly in, attracted by the prospect of a mate. I pick their golden bodies from the soapy water.

At night my son cries. His school shorts are never white. Not white like the other kids' shorts are. He says the washing machine is dumb and living in the bush is dumb.

Fisher & Paykel. Front loader. Overhead a dryer. I ring Mama, offer to do her washing. She says her washing machine is faster than mine. That night I dream of my grandma. Here she is, talking to her neighbour over the fence. 'My copper is very good,' she says. 'I can get it to boil in half the time it takes yours …'

Fisher & Paykel. Quick Smart. Energy rating 3. I am renovating the bush house. The washing machine washes and spin dries with ease. I hang the damp sheets on the line, strung between two trees. Prop it up high with a mānuka stick to catch the wind. The sheets lift and billow over the lawn. When I look again the line is full of little children's clothes. I hardly know myself, nappies fluttering over the ferns.

Accounts of girls raised by swans

Okrug

We swim like foster children, our necks held high, we swim with open arms knowing water will always want us back, we swim like brides with beautiful feet, we swim like Russian thoughts.

We swim in caravans of water, we swim among floating chairs, a toaster, we swim with a lampshade on our heads and when the current surges west, we swim out into the open with the eels.

We swim like we are missed, we swim like we are bridled, we swim under bridges and when the boats come, we swim through scum, through ropes, we swim like rich people, always laughing.

We tap on your window

Dark-dark. Everyone's sleeping. Not us. We smear our lips sticky orange. We put on our black eye masks.

We run into the streets. Our white tutus blaze through the night. *Whoop whoop*!

The men will go crazy for us. The men will say, what do you swan girls want, huh?

We dance for the men. We dance on the lake, so beautiful, we dance.

We fold over. *Splash-splash*. Our Bolshoi legs in the air.

We are swamp potatoes. We are thirsty wild. We are clean as paper.

We steal your women's lipstick. We glissade in their flower beds. Peck holes in their pansies.

Hawnk, hawnk, we laugh.

Dark-dark. Outside your window. We stretch up our long necks. *Tap, tap.*

SS Anakyrna

After the fight, after they called us *waterfowl,* we jumped ship. Onward to America! The foamy bounce of the waves taking us to shore.

We didn't believe in sharks. We believed in inflatables though. And ropes. And each other.

It was cold and wild in that sea. My sister kept screaming. Then she'd lay her head on the orange life buoy and laugh.

'What's that? What's that?' she kept saying.

I told her to keep swimming. I told her I could see America. I told her we were swan girls; water would always hold us.

When she saw the lights, she told me she loved me. 'We did it!' she screamed.

I didn't tell her it was the coastal boat, come searching.

Didn't say us swan girls were swamped.

Language

I want to ask Kenny about our future, like how long do I have to wait before I can call myself his *fiancée*, but he keeps on about his rat problem; how he's going to write a note, asking them to leave his house and I say, 'Listen, they could be Norway rats, they won't understand English, have you thought about that, Kenny, and what you really need is to get some *Warfarin*,' but Kenny says he doesn't want a hand in any sort of killing and when the rats start sending him messages down the radio waves, Kenny packs his suitcase and we wait on the bed for someone from the pysch team to arrive and I rub his back the way he likes it and I think of what I'm going to say to the nurse just so she knows, *I have a medical background*, I know what I'm talking about, it's not just chemical because if it were the lithium would hold him and he wouldn't be *rapid cycling* but I don't get a chance because as soon as they arrive Kenny jumps up with his suitcase and he's in the van and I'm left alone in his house with the rats grinding their teeth and I'm not allowed to see Kenny for three whole days and when I do meet him at the hospital entrance he's wearing white trousers and a red spotted scarf around his neck like he's about to sail away somewhere and he tells me he's been swapping clothes with his mates and he shouts out excitedly when he sees them come out on the lawn and I can see Kenny's got his own social life going on in there ... so I don't give him the grapes I brought, and when I tell him I'm leaving, Kenny does a little bow, *as you wish*, but the thing is, two weeks later he's phoning me up, asking about the rats and in the next breath saying I have to marry him otherwise he'll *blow my fucking brains out.*

Alan Bennett striding over the shore

Maybe it's a short cut to somewhere
and if he keeps walking

out of the photograph and into my room
we'll have a laugh

about our terrible mothers — their warnings
about what was coming to you,

their cheerfulness at the rude disasters
of the world, the train wrecks, the ghosts

of the tsunami leaving a wet patch
on the kitchen chair, *you should*

always carry a penny, a cracker
in your handbag in case you tumble

down the stairs. I imagine he's walking
to get away from the trickiness

of language. A stiff sea breeze to carry
away any stray vowels

so I won't ask him in. Let the mothers float,
their arms splayed to the sky,

let him find the rhythm of his own sure feet.

The knocker-upper

They call me the human clock, but there's a man I can't rouse at No. 19, though I'm paid to rouse him and he's to show himself at the window so I have proof he's been roused, has heard the scatter shot of peas over the pane and sometimes I'll be standing there on the cobbles, blowing my pipe up at the window, my poor lungs heaving with the effort, but still, at my age, bang up to the elephant, every time, and yet no sign he's woken and already the first factory whistles going off and there's nought I can do, there's two more workers on the lane to rouse, No. 30, who appears naked at the window, still clutching his noodle, before disappearing, and then my blind boy, the lad who meets the boats with his barrow, who promises me a basket of herrings, whose hands wander over my face, who tells me that if I can't rouse No. 19 then no one can and for a moment we exchange daft promises, and I'm emboldened he can't see my plain face and '*I will rouse you morning and night*,' I whisper and if this makes a stuffed bird laugh then it's no more preposterous than a man paying good money to a knocker-upper when he's clearly on a downer and quite possibly ready to feed to the fishes.

The fame of Mr Whippy and the crayfish

We last saw Mr Whippy out at sea. The tide had come in fast and Mr Whippy was on the cab roof of his van. Not waving, just sitting there as if he was trying to make sense of his unmoored world. The next day the ice cream van had gone but Mr Whippy was treading water. It was hard getting a boat out but everyone said Mr Whippy looked in good shape and he'd be rescued as soon as things calmed down a bit. The next day Mr Whippy was gone. We ran along the cliff edge, calling out his name but only the gulls cried back.

On the third day of Mr Whippy's disappearance he was sighted again by the rescue helicopter. The weather was too stormy to winch a man down but they leaned out and took a video of Mr Whippy. He was clutching a crayfish. On the TV news it showed Mr Whippy with an arrow pointing right at the shelled creature on his chest. *Mr Whippy, not alone* it read.

On the fifth day Mr Whippy was floating on his back. His face looked pretty salt bitten. The crayfish was still with him and in the video you could see it's black beady eyes looking at Mr Whippy, an antenna flailing close to his nose.

At night everyone rushed to their TVs to watch the updates of Mr Whippy and co. They looked so small in that vast ocean. Mr Whippy could be heard singing to the crayfish. The crayfish waved its hard bristly legs in the air. Waves slopped over them. 'That crayfish is hanging on,' we said. 'That crayfish is not gonna leave him.'

We all knew without food and water, things were looking pretty grim.

On the last day there was a particularly poignant moment. Mr Whippy held the crayfish up in the air and told the crayfish he'd never forget him. 'I'm sorry, bud,' he gasped, 'sorry.' We thought we heard a snapping noise, a slurp, and then the screen went blank. They'd pulled the story off air.

We were holding our breath for that crayfish. We knew there'd always be a Mr Whippy, up the street, down the street, in whatever suburb you lived, but that particular crayfish with the black beady eyes, that particular one that flailed its tender antenna in front of Mr Whippy's nose, that one made us hungry for something more noble than ourselves.

CODA

After Mr Whippy was finally rescued, he went back to selling ice creams. But the once perfect twirl on his cones never did reach the same heights. He'd stare out the van to where the beach crowds used to be. The TV show tried to get another series on him. *Man Eats Friend.* Mr Whippy shook his head. His pale eyes scanned the sky. 'More storms coming,' he said.

How we scare ourselves

Everyone likes a good scare, a spin on a roller coaster or a drive right to the edge of the cliff, waves crashing below and gulls screaming like their throats are being slit, so when my sister drives off with Ricky in his new Mustang, I just know he'll want to scare her, maybe by closing his eyes tight while he drives fast down Long Plain Road, maybe by stopping right under Hangman's Rock that looms over the road and him saying, 'All that hazard tape around the base could sure come in handy for tying something up,' and in this way I scare myself more than Ricky could ever scare my sister because already I have Ricky blindfolding her with tape, tying up her wrists, saying, 'Honey if you really love me keep walking towards the cliff. Until I say stop.' And my poor love-smitten sister starts walking towards the precipice, the ends of the red tape fluttering behind her.

They'll have a baby, of course. My sister will be so thankful she's still alive she'll let Ricky do anything to her. She'll be thinking, *what the hell* and *you only live once*. But then I realise I'll never see her again, Ricky will drive her away, far up north to live and this is where it no longer suits me to scare myself with these thoughts and this is why later, when the dogs start barking, car dust billowing down the road, I turn up the music, I start dancing by the window so they can see me, a girl who's not afraid of anything, a girl that screeches like a gull when they walk through the door.

Crabs

the paddle crabs tend to move to deeper
water as they age. there they lie submerged
in sediment only the eyes, the antennae
exposed
how I love
the word, carapace, the light red terracotta of shell
my finger tracing the sharp serrations
the claws of stubble, so stiff
my mouth is an ocean of foam

When Kaiwhakaruaki comes

Me and Bobby under an upturned dinghy on the beach, trying to get it off with each other, but overcome with laughter and lying there in a sandy tangle, outside the night coming down, the sigh and heave of the ocean and Bobby saying, 'How many other men have you had?' and me saying, 'I could count the fingers on one hand,' and saying, 'What about you?' and kind of bracing myself as if to hear bad news and kind of thinking, *why do we even ask these dumb questions* and in the silence that's when I heard something change in the water and, 'Listen,' I say to Bobby and Bobby listens and something is out there, maybe a boat coming to shore, maybe a dredger, the nets being hauled in but 'No,' Bobby says, 'That's a different noise.' He grabs my shoulder and *taniwha* he breathes into my neck and I squirm away and *taniwha* Bobby breathes into my ear and I just about scream at the thought of a monster reptile out there and then I tell Bobby it's actually his wife out looking for him and Bobby says, 'What wife?' and then I say, 'What taniwha?' and we go on like this for a while and then Bobby says he didn't realise how cold the sand got at night and his leg is getting a bit cramped up and I say, 'Do you want to quit this?' and Bobby says, 'No, we'll sleep here tonight, if that's what you want,' and the thing is I don't know what

I want right now. I do know my friends would say it was legend that Bobby and me slept under an upturned dinghy on Parapara beach when there was something out there in the water but another voice in my head and this is my Nanny's voice says, 'You get gone, girl.'

Later I will try and explain Bobby's disappearance. How I ran off and Bobby, curious about the big wave, stayed behind. But my throat has been scoured clean of words. If my Nanny was alive she'd say, 'Kaiwhakaruaki, must have smelled human flesh, must have flicked its tail, excitedly, and *whoosh*, a mighty wave sped towards the shore. Only a heahea boy would stay behind, his gob hung open with wonder.'

But that is later. Right now Bobby is trying to quieten me with his body, his feet digging into the sand, his hands on my shoulders. 'You are my number one girl,' he breathes. In the cramped space, I turn my head to listen.

Notes

When old fiddlers fall off their stools

This references the tradition of throwing wrapped pennies to wandering fiddlers. The line 'Respect! They are artists, not beggars' has been adapted from a line in an essay on Marc Chagall's *Le Violiniste Bleu* by Diana Leo.

Jennie Worgan, the Midge's housewife

This title was taken from the 1904 original billing advertising the Midget City in Dreamland, Coney Island. The city, sometimes known as Lilliputia, was a community of three hundred people who came to Dreamland to live in an experimental community. Jennie Worgan was house keeper to the famous General Tom Thumb.

The boy who grew antlers

This carries echoes of the poem, 'The boy changed into a stag clamors at the gate of secrets' by Ferenc Juhász.

The laughing epidemic

Wikipedia reports that the Tanganyika laughter epidemic of 1962 began as an outbreak of mass hysteria in a girl's boarding school and quickly spread to neighbouring schools. In all, fourteen schools were shut down.

Seeing Stan

This is a sequel to the story 'Truthful Lies', which was published in *Sport 22* (Autumn 1999) and *Flash Fiction International: Very Short Stories from Around the World*, edited by James Thomas, Robert Shapard and Christopher Merrill (WW Norton, 2015).

A litany of the washing machines in my life

I was inspired to write this after reading an article 'A litany of failed homes' which encompasses 'The trouble with all the houses I've lived in' by Lucia Berlin, *The Paris Review*, 2018.

The knocker-upper

According to Wikipedia, 'A knocker-up, sometimes known as a knocker-upper, was a member of a profession in Britain and Ireland that started during, and lasted well into, the Industrial Revolution, when alarm clocks were neither cheap nor reliable. A knocker-up's job was to rouse sleeping people so they could get to work on time.'

When Kaiwhakaruaki comes

Kaiwhakaruaki, the taniwha, inhabited the Parapara Inlet in Mohua Golden Bay, Aotearoa New Zealand. Heahea is te reo Māori for stupid, silly, idiotic.

Acknowledgements

Thanks to my Ōtautahi writing groups and writing friends including Zoë Meager, Meg Pokrass, Leanne Radojkovich, Lynn Davidson and special mention to Nicholas Williamson who often has to stop what he's doing to listen to my endless readings.

Thanks to Catherine Montgomery, publisher at Canterbury University Press. I am enormously grateful for her continued support and belief in my writing. Thanks also to Emma Neale for her excellent editorial advice. Finally, a big thank you to Aaron Beehre (book designer) and Katrina McCallum (editor at Canterbury University Press).

Grateful acknowledgement is made to the editors and publishers of the magazines and anthologies in which the following works, or earlier versions of them, first appeared: a version of 'Magdalene, the sister we could not fathom' was published in *The Phare* (2021); 'The wandering nature of us girls' was previously published in *The Phare* (2021); 'Swimming with Cliff' was previously published in *Flash Boulevard* (2021); 'The winter swimming of my grandmother' was previously published in *New Flash Fiction Review* (2021); 'Steadfast's breath' was previously published in *Atticus Review* (March 2021); 'Stories told on the swings' was previously published in *Atticus Review* (March 2021); 'Chase' was previously published in *X-R-A-Y Literary Magazine* (October 2021); 'Romance in the lower and upper atmosphere' was previously published in *Atticus Review* (March 2021); 'Explaining the *Sputnik* dog to my child' was previously published in the *Pale Fire: New writing on the moon anthology* (Frogmore Press, 2019); 'Laugh, Doreen' was previously published as 'Taking turns' in *Flash Boulevard* (April 2021); 'Walk, run' was previously published in *New World Writing* (April. 2021); 'The ring master's boys' was previously published in *Atticus Review* (October 2020); 'The milk-bottle legs of the high-wire woman' was previously published in *X-R-A-Y Literary Magazine* (September 2020); 'Johnny Owl' was previously published in *Atticus Review* (October 2020);

'What baby wants' was previously published in *New World Writing* (April 2021); 'The undetectable mystery of my husband's illness' was previously published in *Turbine/Kapohau* (2019); 'The uprising of my aunt' is due to be published in *No Other Place to Stand: An anthology of climate change poetry from Aotearoa New Zealand* (Auckland University Press, 2022); 'We, the school dental nurses, 1960' was previously published in *Flashback Fiction* (February 2021); 'The elephant in the room' was previously published in *New Flash Fiction Review* (2021); a version of 'The girl from the laundromat' was published in *New Flash Fiction Review* (April 2021); 'Hunting my father's voice, County Down' first appeared as a Phantom Bill sticker poem Autumn series (2015); a version of 'Horse love' was published in *New World Writing* (April 2021); a version of 'Madame Yeti' was published in *Fictive Dream* (February 2020); 'Our uncles, us girls' was previously published in *The Blue Nib* (June 2020); 'What extremely muscular horses can teach us about climate change' was previously published in *Landfall* (November 2021); 'The existential crab colony of Kyushu Bay' was previously published in *Jaam32* (2013); a version of 'Seven starts to the tumbling of Annie Edson' was published as 'Seven starts to the woman who went over the falls in a barrel' in *Cleaver* (September 2021); the first part of 'Accounts of girls raised by swans' was previously published as 'Girls raised by swans' in Paula Green's *NZ Poetry Shelf* (October 2021); 'Alan Bennett striding over the shore' was previously published in *Jaam32* (2013); and 'Crabs' was previously published in *The Phare* (August 2021).